MR DOG

AND THE SEAL DEAL

BEN FOGLE

with Steve Cole

Illustrated by Nikolas Ilic

HarperCollins *Children's Books*

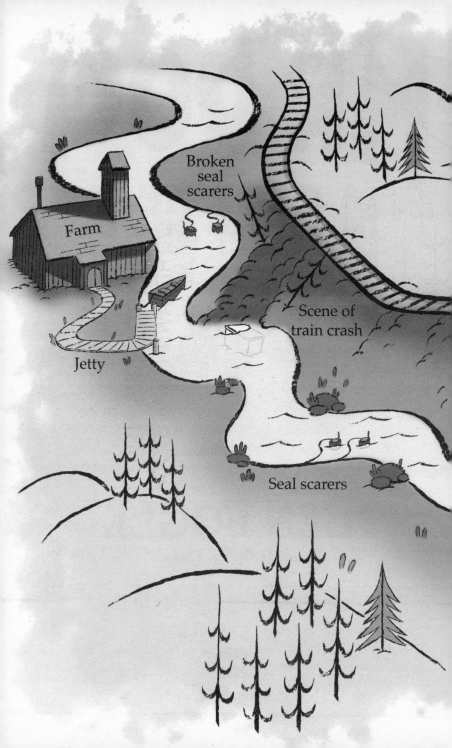

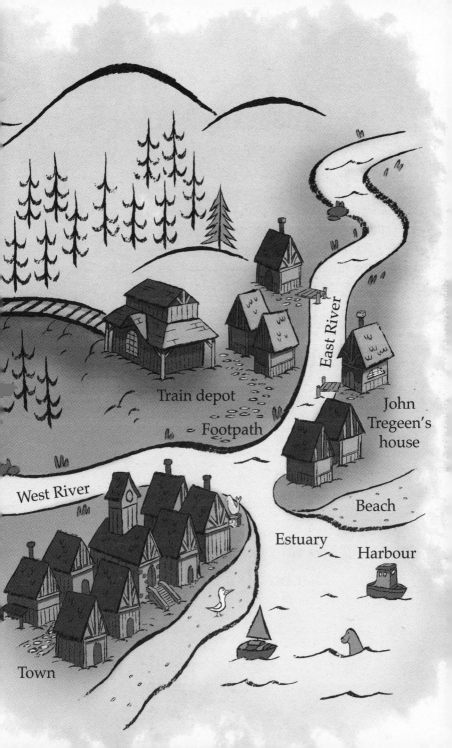

Train depot

Footpath

East River

John Tregeen's house

West River

Beach

Estuary

Harbour

Town

About the Author

BEN FOGLE is a broadcaster and seasoned adventurer. A modern-day nomad and journeyman, he has travelled to more than a hundred countries and accomplished amazing feats; from swimming with crocodiles to rowing three thousand miles across the Atlantic Ocean; from crossing Antarctica on foot to surviving a year as a castaway on a remote Hebridean island. Most recently, Ben climbed Mount Everest. Oh, and he LOVES dogs.

Books by Ben Fogle

MR DOG AND THE RABBIT HABIT

MR DOG AND THE SEAL DEAL

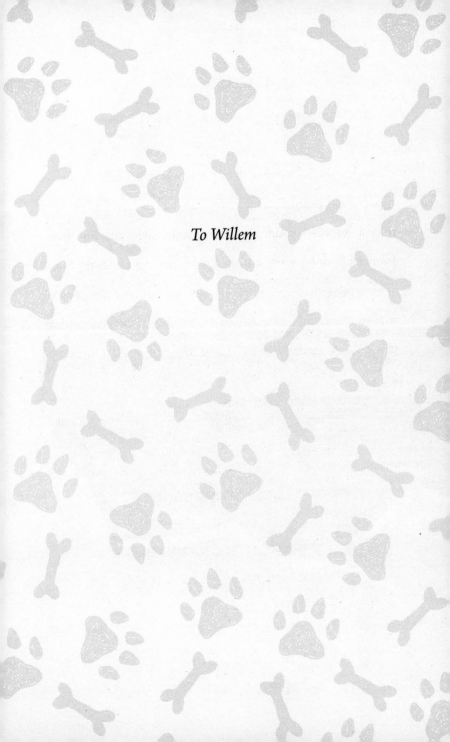

To Willem

Chapter One

WHO'S DITZY?

'Ahhh! A life on the waves for me!' Mr Dog stood on the deck of the fishing boat as it chugged towards the harbour and breathed the salty sea air. His dark, scraggy fur was ruffled by the summer wind, and his white front paws rested on a fishing basket crammed with catches fresh from the ocean. 'I made a good choice allowing a fisherman to look after me! Yes, a very good choice indeed.'

Mr Dog loved travel and adventure. He had no real home and no single owner, but he let people take him in now and again as he travelled from place to place. The boat's skipper, John Tregeen, was the latest to be won over by the roaming animal's special scruffy appeal. Mr Dog turned to him now, raised his shaggy eyebrows and wagged his long tail furiously, hoping for a treat. In place of a collar he had a red-and-white hanky tied round his neck.

There were so

many delicious fish on the boat, surely one could

be spared for a hungry hound . . .?

John Tregeen, who was tall, fair and red-

cheeked, smiled with one hand on the tiller,

steering them home. 'Sorry, dog. These fish are

going up for sale, not down a mutt's gullet!' He

pulled a bone-shaped biscuit from his pocket and

tossed it over. 'How's this instead?'

Expertly, Mr Dog

caught the treat

and crunched it

quickly. *Mmm,*

not bad, he

thought. *But one*

3

treat is never enough! He danced on his back legs to encourage the skipper to throw another.

His plan worked! Another treat came sailing through the air . . .

And a white blur swooped down and snatched it!

'Hey!' Mr Dog frowned at a seagull as it landed on the other side of the boat and the treat vanished down its yellow beak.

John laughed. 'Too slow, my friend.'

'That was mine!' Mr Dog told the seagull.

'Sorry, old sport,' the bird replied with a screech. 'Finders keepers. There's not much food to be had on the beach today; the humans are cleaning it up.'

'Are they, indeed?' Curious, Mr Dog forgot his stomach and looked towards the golden beach. It nestled at the bottom of a large sloping hill that showed off the town's streets and houses to the sea. There were lots of children holding black bin liners down on the sand, some of them with grabbers on the end of sticks, while adults watched and organised.

'They're picking up everything,' said the gull. 'Rope, bits of net, fishing lines . . . and plenty of the plastic rubbish that washes up on the shore.'

'That's good,' said Mr Dog. 'That pollution makes a mess and hurts animals.'

'True.' The gull nodded. 'It's just a shame they

clear up all of the food that's been left behind too.'

'I think you'd better make yourself scarce,' Mr Dog warned the gull as one of John's two-man crew – a skinny young man named Sadiq – waved an arm to shoo the bird away.

With a shrug, the gull spread his wings and soared across the harbour to perch on a red tugboat.

Mr Dog was about to raise his paws for a further biscuit when he noticed a smooth head bob up from the water beside the tug. The head was mottled grey and white with dark round eyes, and whiskers that went in all directions.

'Goodness,' Mr Dog woofed quietly, 'that's a real seal if ever I saw one – which I haven't until this moment!'

The seal looked up at the gull. 'No news of Ditzy, I suppose?'

The gull shook his head. 'No one's seen Ditzy around here. Not for a long time.'

Ditzy? Mr Dog twitched an ear. *Who's Ditzy, I wonder?*

'I really hope someone finds her,' said the seal glumly. Then its head plopped back beneath the water, the gull flew away and John Tregeen was holding out another crunchy snack.

Taking no chances this time, Mr Dog scampered over on his hind legs and snaffled the treat straight from the skipper's hand. 'People often tell me I take the biscuit,' Mr Dog panted happily, sitting back down. 'And they're right!'

John slowed the engine to a throaty *put-put-put* as the boat neared the jetty. Sadiq jumped aboard to secure the craft while the other man

8

began to unload crates of fish. John and his friends would take the haul to market now, so restaurants could stock up for the evening with fresh cod and flounder. With a bark of farewell, Mr Dog jumped on to the jetty and left them to it, weaving his way through holidaymakers heading for the beach.

'It's a splendid afternoon for cleaning up the sand,' he declared, 'and since the "Mister" in my name is almost certainly short for "Never *missed a* chance to help", I'd better join in!'

As he trotted along, Mr Dog noticed the statue of a large one-eyed seal that stood – or lay – on a rock across the harbour. Mr Dog had heard that this celebrated character had lived for years on a nearby island and had regularly entered the harbour to entertain the tourists. Seals seemed to be well loved around these parts. But who or what was the mysterious Ditzy – and where had Ditzy gone?

Just then, Mr Dog caught sight of a gannet plunging from the sky like a javelin into the harbour; perhaps it had spotted a fish that had been thrown back in the water from one of the boats? There was a younger gannet, her wings not yet as pure white as her mother's, pecking and paddling in the creamy shallow wash where the tide met the beach. Mr Dog frowned to see the rubbish in the water there, not yet collected.

Suddenly, Mr Dog saw the young gannet shake her head wildly and hop about in distress. He could see that there was something caught in her beak – something she couldn't shift.

Mr Dog gasped. The gannet had swallowed part of a plastic bag – and now it was stuck in her throat!

Chapter Two

TO THE RESCUE!

'Hold on, young bird!' called Mr Dog.

The gannet was too busy choking to fly away as Mr Dog ran up. Carefully, he gripped the wisp of white plastic with the tips of his teeth and tugged it out from the gannet's beak. Phew! The bird could breathe again!

'Puh!' Mr Dog spat the bit of bag out on to the wet sand. 'How unpleasant.'

The adult gannet appeared with a warning cry, hissing and waving her wings to scare Mr Dog away from her child.

'No need for alarm!' Mr Dog protested. 'I was helping your little one.'

The young gannet nodded quickly. 'It's true!'

13

Mr Dog held down the bit of bag with a paw. 'This perishing plastic is a proper peril, isn't it?'

The mother gannet sighed. 'There's so much of it. And when the river flooded a while back it seemed to get much worse.'

'Oh?' Mr Dog raised a shaggy eyebrow. 'Why's that?'

'Search me,' said the gannet.

'I thought that bit of bag was a fish,' said the young bird sadly. 'I got mixed up.'

'Easily done,' Mr Dog assured her. 'Now, I'm going to help these young humans clean up the place so it can't happen again.'

The mother gannet looked at him. 'You are a

14

kind dog. I wish I could help you in return.'

'Hmm, perhaps you can,' said Mr Dog. 'Do you know anything about someone called Ditzy?'

'Ditzy!' the young gannet piped up. 'She's a seal!'

'A very friendly and popular seal,' the mother gannet agreed. 'She used to show off in the harbour every day . . . then one day, a couple of months ago, she disappeared.'

'And no one has spotted her since?' mused Mr Dog.

The mother gannet jabbed her beak back towards the estuary where a river spilled into the harbour. 'Well, last week, some seabirds I know said they'd seen a small dark seal swimming inland, up the river. But that doesn't sound like Ditzy. Ditzy was big and grey with darker spots on her face and neck.'

'It was probably just a dog they saw,' the young gannet said.

'*Just* a dog?' Mr Dog pretended to look scandalised.

'Everyone here misses Ditzy,' the mother went on, 'including us birds. A lot of tourists came here just to see her, and we would enjoy the food they left behind.'

'I would love to find her,' said Mr Dog. 'I do enjoy a mystery, you know. Why, the "*Mister*"

16

part of my name is short for "mystery"!'

'Is it really?' asked the young gannet.

'Maybe.' Mr Dog's jaws widened in a doggy grin. 'That's a mystery too.' He looked across the beach as two girls with buckets headed their way. 'It seems we have company – *clean-up* company! I must help them tidy this beach before there are any more accidents.'

'Well, thank you again, Mr Dog!' said the mother gannet and, with a screech and a stretch of wings, the gannet and her youngster took off into the sky.

Mr Dog picked up the strip of white plastic with his teeth, padded across the golden sand to

the children and placed it carefully into the older

girl's bucket.

'Clever boy!' the girl said, grinning. 'You're

Mr Tregeen's new dog, aren't you?'

You're almost right, thought Mr Dog with a

woof. *Mr Tregeen's my new person!*

'Do you think he's a hunting dog?' the girl's friend wondered. 'If he is, maybe *he* could find Ditzy.'

'I wish someone would.' The girl shrugged sadly, and they walked away to pick up some more rubbish. 'The harbour simply isn't the same without Ditzy splashing about . . .'

More locals missing Ditzy, thought Mr Dog, watching them go. *That girl called me clever, which is quite true . . . But am I clever enough to solve the mystery of the missing seal?* He padded over to a plastic coffee-cup lid and picked it up in his teeth. *I suppose there's only one way to find out. Once this clean-up is out of the way, it's time for an adventure!*

That summer evening, as the blue sky drifted
into grey, Mr Dog lay in the ramshackle
old kennel in John Tregeen's garden. He'd
worked hard on the beach, enjoyed a delicious
meal of rice and fish afterwards and now he
was napping to keep up his energy levels.
Tonight, while it was cool and quiet, he would
begin his expedition to find the missing
Ditzy!

John Tregeen opened the back door of his
cottage and peered out at the kennel. 'You
there, boy? Coming inside?'

Mr Dog rose, stretched and went over to

the fisherman. He pressed himself against John's legs to say thank you for his lodging, then turned and padded away to the garden gate.

John smiled. 'Is it time to say goodbye?'

For now, thought Mr Dog. He gave a quiet woof of farewell to the man in the moonlight, then turned and trotted away on to the footpath that ran alongside the row of fishermen's cottages. Ahead of him, the sea was silvery dark as it stirred and shifted in the breeze, bobbing the boats in the harbour. The cries of night birds sounded in the distance.

Mr Dog was heading for the estuary, where

the river merged with the sea. Then he would

follow the course of the river inland. The

search for Ditzy had begun!

Chapter Three

A CRY FOR HELP

Mr Dog wandered through the woodland that ran alongside the river. At first, the water in the river had been salty and no good to drink. But in the middle of that first night, it had started to rain hard. Thunder had crackled through the darkness. Mr Dog huddled under a tree and watched the rainwater stream from fleshy leaves. He lay on his back, opened his mouth and rolled about from side to side, drinking his fill and enjoying his freedom.

The storm didn't stop until well into the next morning. The sky looked heavy, weighed down with grey clouds. Mr Dog continued his journey. Happily, he walked along the waterlogged riverbank. The river split in two, with one branch twisting out of sight to the east, while a wider branch wound round to the west. Mr Dog decided that west was best, and off he went.

Around lunchtime, he met a fisherman who was sitting at the side of the river. From the looks of things he hadn't caught any fish, and he was gloomily eating a ham sandwich.

Mr Dog danced on his back legs in the hope of a donation, but the fisherman ignored him, and so he went on his way. 'Can't win them all,' he told himself, and trotted onwards as the sun moved steadily through the sky.

Late that afternoon, Mr Dog saw a gannet about to eat a fish. 'I say,' he called, 'I don't suppose any of you birds have seen a seal about?'

The bird stopped to consider. 'I saw something like a fat grey sausage swimming up the river . . .' But then another bird swooped in and stole the fish, and the gannet took off to give chase. The conversation was over.

As it grew dark, Mr Dog settled for the night in a cosy patch of woodland and was up again at dawn. For a while, he followed a railway line that ran alongside the river, but then a heavy goods train came rumbling by, letting off smelly fumes, so Mr Dog returned to the riverbank. Much to his annoyance, he found bits of plastic wrapping caught in the reeds there. The mother gannet on the beach had said that the floods a while back had made more plastic appear . . . but how?

'Another mystery,' he murmured. Quickly, he dug a hole in the wet earth and buried the plastic out of the way.

*

The rain started again
that afternoon and
came down harder
and harder. Mr
Dog continued his
journey along the
river, as it widened
here and grew
thinner there, until
evening fell. Wet and
cold, he retreated
into the woodland

that ran along the riverbank for cover and thought longingly of the kennel at John Tregeen's house. He heard the lonely clank and rattle of a train trundling through the night, and as the echoes faded he heard a stranger noise. It was a sort of grunting bark, but in no dog language that he recognised.

'Whatever is making that noise?'

Mr Dog's curiosity led him back out into the downpour. The grunting and squealing sounded more urgent, like someone was in distress. The noise was coming from beyond the forest, somewhere along the river. Mr Dog hurried out from the bracken and nettles to investigate.

'Hello?' he howled.

A reply rose over the echoes of his call: 'Over here!' It was a high, throaty voice. 'I'm stuck!'

The sky had darkened. Lightning flashed, unleashing the thunder's crackle and roar. The rain rang down on the shimmering river. Mr Dog shook water from his fur and pressed on along the riverbank. 'Keep calling! I'll find you . . .'

Soon he saw something wriggling on the riverbank: a sleek, smooth figure, bundled in blubber. The animal was dark grey with wide black eyes and looked tired and scared. Two stubby webbed flippers, with a claw on each tiny toe, waggled helplessly from its chest. There were bristly whiskers across the snout that pushed out from its face. The animal was struggling, as if in some invisible embrace.

'Aha – a seal!' cried Mr Dog. 'Found you at last.'

'A dog!' cried the animal in surprise, sliding slowly back into the water. 'Why are you looking for me?'

'Because you've been missing! Ditzy, isn't it? I'm so happy to find you!'

'Ditzy?' The seal's eyes widened further. 'Oh, no, no, no. I'm not Ditzy. I'm called Lulu. Ditzy's my friend. I've been looking for her.'

'Have you indeed? Well, that makes two of us.'

Mr Dog remembered the gannets saying some seabirds had sighted a small grey seal inland – it must have been Lulu that they'd seen! 'Well, it's nice to meet you, Lulu. My name is Mr Dog.'

'Hello, Mr Dog,' said Lulu. 'Are you a friend of Ditzy's too?'

'I'm a friend to any animal in trouble,' Mr Dog declared, 'including you. Now, whatever's wrong?'

'I'm caught! Snagged! Stuck!' Lulu wriggled again. 'I was chasing a fish when I got tangled in something, and now I can't get out!'

'Let's have a look,' said Mr Dog.

As he approached, Lulu struggled again to

32

pull herself further up on to the riverbank. Mr Dog could see there was something thin and red digging into the fat dark-grey sausage of the seal's body just beneath the water, holding her back. 'That looks like a net,' he concluded. 'A bit of broken fishing net.'

'It's caught on something,' Lulu gasped. 'I'm totally stuck. Fixed. Grounded.'

'Let me see what I can do.' Mr Dog took a breath and then drove his nose into the water. The net looked to be tangled round something sticking out from the riverbed. He bit at the plastic strands, trying to slice through the tough fibres, and tugged at them with his claws.

Ouch! he thought, getting nowhere.

Lightning flashed again and the rain fell harder still. Panting for breath, Lulu lay still on her side, only her head free of the river. 'What am I going to do?'

Mr Dog didn't answer. *If the river continues to swell like this, poor Lulu will be trapped underwater,* he thought, *and seals can't live without air to breathe.* He thrust his chops down into the water again and chewed at the netting. *If I can't set Lulu free, she'll drown!*

Chapter Four

A TANGLED TALE

Mr Dog pulled his head from the water, panting for breath. 'I'm sorry, Lulu.' There was a soft whine behind his words. 'The netting is really strong. I can't break it . . .'

'I'm finished, aren't I?' Lulu groaned. 'I'm doomed and done for. I'm sunk!'

'Sunk . . .' Mr Dog thought hard, then gave a loud bark of excitement. 'Wait a moment, Lulu – that might be it. The net's got tangled in something that's sunk into the riverbed. If I can't break the net, perhaps I can dig out whatever it's wrapped round!'

'Ingenious!' Lulu twittered. 'What a smart dog you are.'

'You're absolutely right!' Mr Dog gave her a doggy grin. 'I can see you and I will make great friends.'

The lightning flashed again and Lulu quivered, her blubber wobbling. 'Please, Mr Dog. Hurry!'

Mr Dog took a deep breath, then plunged

his head down into the cold, dark water beside

Lulu. He couldn't see a thing, but ran his snout

over the net, following it down to where it had

snagged in the riverbed. His front paws sank into

thick mud and he started to dig. It wasn't easy in

the cold water – the sludge was as thick as treacle.

Mr Dog's heart was beating hard against his ribs

as he dug and dug . . .

Lulu was straining and struggling, inching

further up the bank. 'I . . . I think it's working.'

Mr Dog tore with his paws at the thick mud.

There was a piece of wood wedged into the

riverbed. As Mr Dog dug deeper, he could see

that the net was wrapped round it. Finally it came

loose and Lulu gave a squeal of freedom. She wriggled and slithered up the riverbank on her belly, the net still wrapped tightly round her like a strange swimsuit. Mr Dog led her over to the cover of a nearby tree and lay down beside her as the rain fell. Both animals were panting hard.

Lulu saw that her rescuer was shivering, so she nuzzled up beside him. 'Thank you,' she grunted softly.

'I might have to change my name from Mr Dog to Mr *Dig*.' He looked at her. 'Are you all right?'

Lulu stretched her body and then gasped. 'I must've twisted a flipper trying to get free. And this net has cut into my skin . . .'

Mr Dog saw red scratches on the seal's hide. As delicately as he could, he unravelled the netting and pulled it free. 'That's strange,' he said, studying the bright-red fibres. 'I thought the net would be old rubbish the humans had thrown into the river. But this looks new. Perhaps it fell off a boat?'

'Wherever it came from, it's very dangerous.' Lulu shivered. 'Oh, I do hope Ditzy hasn't got caught in one too. I've been so worried about her.'

Mr Dog nodded. 'Is she a really good friend of yours?'

'I've known her since we were pups,' said Lulu. 'I'm a lot shyer than she is, though. I couldn't show off to the humans in the harbour like her. One day, months ago, she said she was going to explore the river – but no one has heard from her since. I do hope she's all . . . fish.'

Mr Dog's shaggy eyebrows twitched. 'All fish?'

'Fish!' Lulu's whiskers wobbled as she sniffed the air. 'I smell fish. Do you smell fish?'

Mr Dog sniffed too. 'Well, now that you mention it . . . Yes! There's one there.' He nodded to a large salmon lying on its side in the rain-pattered water near the bank. 'Smells fresh. How did it get there?'

'I caught it earlier – that's how I got tangled up. I must have been sitting on it!' Lulu flexed her flippers and belly-flopped down the slope to claim her catch. 'Care to share? You've earned a reward!'

Soon Lulu was back beneath the tree, gnawing

on the fishy dish that she clutched in her paws and sharing tasty morsels with Mr Dog. 'Ditzy is dotty about salmon, you know,' she said. 'Loves it. Adores it!'

'I quite understand.' Mr Dog licked his chops. 'Are there many salmon in this river?'

'Oh yes, lots – and in the East River too,' said Lulu. 'I've travelled up and down it looking for Ditzy and helping myself!' As Lulu munched some more, Mr Dog saw that the teeth in her jaws were as sharp and white as his own. 'When I was exploring that branch of this river, I met some very kind and helpful humans – they'd caught a lot of fish and left them in a net for me.'

Mr Dog looked at her. 'Those anglers weren't leaving anything for you, Lulu! Those fish were caught for sport, or to eat, or to sell to restaurants.'

'Well, that doesn't sound right.' Lulu swallowed the tail. 'When I took the fish, the anglers jumped up and shouted and shook their fists at me. They were really happy.'

'No, no, Lulu,' said Mr Dog.

'That's what they do when they're *angry*.'

'Angry? Oh no.' She rolled on to her side. 'One of them was so happy he pointed a stick at me that went BOOM, just like a firework.'

'Good gracious.' Mr Dog flattened his ears to his head. 'Lulu, he fired a gun at you. He must've been a hunter. You could have been killed!'

'Killed?' Lulu's black eyes grew wider. 'Why on earth would he want to do that? Humans don't own the fishes. Why can't they share?'

'Some humans are not very good at sharing. Even so, I am very surprised they shot at you.' Mr Dog thought hard. 'Something serious must have happened around here. I wonder what?'

'Perhaps Ditzy will know. I hope I find her on

this stretch of the river.' Lulu paused. 'I also hope I find another fish. Excuse me while I look for one.'

Mr Dog watched Lulu go back out into the rain, bouncing awkwardly down the sloping bank and into the water. He sighed. He'd discovered one seal, but Ditzy's fate was still unknown. Had hunters found her? Or was she still out there somewhere, looking for Lulu? Perhaps Ditzy had been hurt by rubbish in the water as well?

This mystery is growing deeper, thought Mr Dog, *and more dangerous too!*

Chapter Five

SEAL SPOTTING

As the night wore on, Mr Dog was finally lulled to sleep by the sound of the rain. He was woken in the morning as a train rumbled by, blowing its whistle like an alarm call. The rain had stopped and the sun was trying to shine through the blank white sky.

'Good morning, Mr Dog!' As Lulu wiggled back up the bank towards him, she tossed a fat, juicy fish in his direction. 'I'm heading off again, upriver. Ditzy's got to be out there somewhere.'

'Tell me, Lulu.' Mr Dog stood up and stretched his scruffy body, dragging his back legs behind him. 'Do seals often leave the sea to swim in rivers?'

'Sometimes if we're chasing after fish . . . we get a bit lost.' Lulu sighed. 'Even so, we don't normally stay longer than a few days.'

'And Ditzy's been gone for a couple of months.' Mr Dog shook his head. 'Well, I'm coming with you to see if we can find her.'

48

'Thank you for helping,' said Lulu.

The unlikely pair set off together. Mr Dog trotted through the long grass at the side of the river, while Lulu beetled about in the water, trying not to use her injured flipper. To pass the time she would sometimes do impressions.

'Hey, look at me.' Lulu lay motionless in the water. 'I'm a log.'

'Very good,' said Mr Dog politely.

She rolled over. 'What am I now?'

'Er, still a log?'

'No. I'm a log WITH A FISH!' She rolled over again to reveal a large salmon gripped in her flippers, and in moments it was gone. 'Mmmm. Nice fish.'

'Look out.' Mr Dog growled a warning. 'Angler!'

Some way up ahead, Mr Dog had spotted a woman with blonde hair sitting on the bank beside an array of rods and nets. She had clearly seen Lulu with the fish. Slowly, carefully, she

reached

into a large

bag beside

her. Mr Dog's

ears pricked and his

hackles rose. Was the woman

a hunter, ready to shoot the

fish-stealing seal? He dropped

to his belly and wriggled through the

grass towards her in an army crawl.

I must get to her in time, he thought. *If I*

jump up at her, I can spoil her aim.

The woman began to pull out something from inside her bag . . . but it was only a mobile phone! The woman started taking pictures of Lulu bobbing about in the water, but as the seal neared the nets placed at the riverside the woman started shaking her head and shouting. She waved angrily as if to scare Lulu away. Quickly, Lulu ducked beneath the water and swam off, and the woman dialled someone on her phone, Mr Dog listening in.

'Hello?' the woman said. 'It's Alana. Listen, you won't believe this, but I've seen that seal you've been after. It's here on the western branch of the river. Went straight for my fish . . . It's gone

now, but seemed to be heading upriver. Yes . . .
yes, I can meet you at the farm . . .'

Mr Dog circled past the woman, heading after Lulu. He didn't like the sound of her conversation. *That seal you've been after,* she'd said. Had she been talking to the hunter who'd taken pot shots at Lulu? Or had the woman mistaken Lulu for Ditzy?

Mr Dog shook his shaggy head. So many questions!

'We must take special care,' Mr Dog told Lulu when he'd caught up with her. 'This is a big river, but it sounds as if some humans are looking for you.'

Lulu's sleek head rose from the water and she stared at Mr Dog with her widest eyes. 'Do you think they've done something to Ditzy?'

'I'm sure people in town would've heard if anything bad had happened to her,' Mr Dog reassured her. 'She was very popular with the people there, as you know. But we should try to find her sooner rather than later so you can both get back to the sea – and safety.'

*

Mr Dog wanted to keep moving and get as far from Alana the angler as they could. But they kept meeting animals who'd come into contact with pollution and needed help. First, they met a duck who'd managed to get a rubber band stuck over his head and jammed between his beak, so he couldn't eat easily. The duck was afraid of Mr Dog and tried to swim away, so Lulu rose from the water beneath him and lifted him up, carrying him back to the riverbank. The duck was so startled that he held still while Mr Dog carefully sliced through the band with his sharpest claw.

Not long after that they came across

something even sadder – a deer with her head

stuck in a plastic jar. The poor deer couldn't see

and hadn't eaten or drunk in some time. Mr Dog

was able to hook his teeth round the rim of the

jar and hold it steady while the deer pulled as

hard as she could. Finally, the deer's head came

free and she tottered down to the bank to drink

thirstily. Mr Dog kicked wet earth into the jar to

fill it and stop any other curious animals from

getting stuck.

'Where's all this horrible waste coming from?'

Mr Dog cried.

'I don't know,' said Lulu, swimming forward,

'but it's being carried downriver to the beach and the harbour, so the source must still be up ahead— AAGH!' The seal gave a squeal of pain and went rigid in the water.

'Lulu? What's wrong?' Mr Dog ran and jumped into the river and swam towards her. He could hear a high-pitched electronic whine beneath the surface and flattened his ears. 'Lulu, what's that horrible sound? Lulu . . .?' He looked all around but he couldn't see the seal. 'Lulu,' he howled, *where are you?*

Chapter Six

DOUBLE DISCOVERY

As suddenly as it had started, the strange electronic siren cut out.

'I'm over here,' said Lulu, rising up from the reeds that grew along the riverbank. 'When I swam away the noise stopped.'

'Perhaps the sound is meant to scare away

seals like you?' Mr Dog joined her on land, shook himself off and peered around. 'Aha!' He stood on his hind legs. 'What's this I spy?'

Lulu looked and saw a thick orange plastic box mounted on a wooden post. A grey cable stretched down from the box into the water.

Mr Dog walked over to investigate.

But when Lulu swam towards it, the sound went off again. 'Ouch!' she grunted. 'There's something down there – something small and orange on the end of that cable. The horrid thing screams every time it sees me!'

'It must be a machine,' said Mr Dog, studying the orange box. 'It can't see you, but perhaps it

has a sensor that *detects* large animals moving
in the river . . . and blasts out that noise to warn
them away.'

As he finished, the noise went off again.
'I didn't go near it that time, though!' Lulu
quivered, hauling herself up on to the riverbank.
'What set it off?'

The blaring noise suddenly cut out
mid-beep. Mr Dog frowned to
see bubbles in the water –
and then, with a great
splash, a dark figure
burst up, making him
jump backwards.

It was another seal, much bigger than Lulu, grey with darker spots on its face and neck. A plastic orange gadget hung uselessly from one end of the cable clamped in its jaws.

'Ditzy!' Lulu clapped her little flippers together as she galumphed down the bank and into the water. 'Ditzy, I've found you!'

'Lulu!' Ditzy rocketed over to meet her and the pair happily knocked noses. 'I'm so happy to see you! I'm glad the seal-scarer didn't frighten you off.' She tossed the cable and box away. It landed by Mr Dog's front paws.

'Seal-scarer?' he echoed.

'Yes, the humans put them in the river to scare us away. But I'm a wee bit deaf so they don't bother me much. I just bite through them – chomp,

chomp, chomp!' Ditzy mimed biting with her big ivory teeth. 'CHOMP! Who are you anyway?'

'My name is Mr Dog. Some say D-O-G is short for Dog of Greatness, but it's not my place to agree.' He grinned and bowed his head. 'I'm very pleased to meet you, Ditzy, but I don't understand why people are going to so much trouble to scare stray seals from this river?'

Lulu blinked. 'Yes, why is that, Ditzy?'

'Come on!' Ditzy gave her a sly smile. 'Don't pretend you don't know. Why else are you here?'

'I'm here because I was worried about you,' said Lulu.

'And I'm here because I enjoy a mystery mixed

up with an adventure,' Mr Dog added. 'But why are *you* here? Why are the humans trying so hard to scare seals away?'

'Why?' Ditzy threw back her head and made a grunting, honking noise like laughter. 'I must show you. Come with me, Lulu. You'll be amazed – and very well fed.'

'Ooooh!' Lulu's black eyes had grown to the size of saucers. 'All right, Ditzy.'

'Wait! Whatever you've found, it could be dangerous,' Mr Dog warned the seals. 'The anglers have set these noisy boxes to keep you away, Ditzy, but you haven't listened – quite literally! You've ignored the warnings and it seems to me that people are ready to take more serious action.'

'Come now, doggy. They wouldn't hurt Ditzy, the celebrated seal!' Ditzy turned in an ungainly circle that made Mr Dog smile despite himself. 'Er, would they?'

'Someone shot at poor Lulu,' Mr Dog informed her.

'Well! I'm sure they didn't mean to.' Ditzy did

65

a blubbery somersault. 'Now come on, Lulu, I simply *must* show you why I've stuck around here for so long.' And with that, she powered away through the water. 'This way. Chop-chop!'

Mr Dog hared off after Ditzy along the riverbank, but he could see that Lulu was finding it harder to keep up.

'Wait for me! I can't go as fast as you, Ditzy,' she said.

But the slightly deaf seal didn't hear her. 'Pardon?'

'I hurt my flipper,' Lulu called.

'You caught a kipper? Good girl!'

'No, she hurt her *flipper* when she got tangled

66

in a piece of net,' Mr Dog explained as he ran

along. 'Perhaps you should stop for a minute?'

'Oh, very well,' Ditzy grumbled.

Just then, Mr Dog caught a high-pitched

metallic vibration from behind him. Looking

about, he saw a jagged gap in the trees and,

beyond that, a railway track. 'A train is coming,'

he observed.

'Oooh, is it? What good timing!' Ditzy

clapped, swam to the bank and wibbled up

the slope towards the train line. 'I'll give the

passengers on board a real performance ... I do

miss putting on a show!'

But, as the train came clanking past, Mr Dog

saw it was only a goods train – an engine pulling

a lot of wagons that carried things, not people.

Ditzy looked disappointed. 'Oh. No audience,

as usual. Just those silly old wagons full of nasty

plastic rubbish.'

'Eh? Plastic rubbish?' Mr Dog stared at her.

'How do you know what's inside those wagons?'

'Because the first time I passed this spot,

something awful happened!' Ditzy galumphed a

little nearer to him. 'Earlier in the summer there

were terrible rains that brought terrible floods.

The tracks were swamped with water and a train

derailed, right here! Its wagons fell over and they

crashed through those trees and tore them down.

68

The noise!' Like all seals, Ditzy's ears were hardly visible, but she shook her head from side to side. 'I couldn't believe it as a big crate fell from one of the wagons and came rolling over and over . . .'

Mr Dog stepped so close to her they were almost nose to nose. 'Ditzy, do you know where that crate is now?'

'In the water over there.' Ditzy nodded to the side of the bank. 'The crate's broken open – so all the nasty plastic stuff inside is getting out!'

Chapter Seven

DELIGHT AND DANGER

'Well, well,' said Mr Dog as Lulu caught them up and came swimming over. 'Finally we know where the plastic's been coming from.' He could see now that the clearing wasn't natural: the trees had been broken down instead of having fallen, and the ground around was scarred and flattened. 'When the train went off the rails, one of the crates must have fallen into the water and sunk out of sight.'

'So it was never found,' Ditzy agreed.

Mr Dog waded into the water and checked out the crate. It was a plastic box as big as a freezer, white and dented with its hinged lid twisted half off. A length of red netting trailed lazily from one sharp corner.

Lulu dipped beneath the water to study it, then bobbed back up. 'Each time there's a flood, more stuff inside is washed out . . .' She waggled her poorly flipper. 'And more animals get hurt.'

Mr Dog nodded sadly. He remembered the deer and the duck. He never wanted to see another creature have to suffer that way. 'There's more of that nasty red netting caught round the lid,' he observed. 'It must have come from inside the crate.'

'Oh, no, no, no, it didn't. I can show you just where that particular net came from – *and* how it got there.' Ditzy had a sly smile on her face again. 'You won't believe what I'm going to show you, Lu. Come on – upriver we go!'

Mr Dog's bushy brows knitted together. *Whatever can she mean?* With a *wait-for-me!* woof, he ran after Ditzy and Lulu as they swam along the river. But his paws felt heavier now he knew

about the crate and how much more rubbish was inside it. *If only we could show someone it's there!* he thought. He hated having to leave the rotten thing to poison the landscape further. But he also knew that the seals might be in danger, so he couldn't leave them alone either.

*

Finally, after what felt like hours, Mr Dog came to a place where the river slowly widened as it wound through the countryside, and signs that read **PRIVATE PROPERTY** and **KEEP OUT** began to sprout like ugly flowers.

Mr Dog ignored them and went on through. 'They can't expect a dog to read,' he said cheerily.

74

The ground was waterlogged, and gleaming pools lay either side of the now familiar railway tracks. Soon Mr Dog could see a large metal framework as long as several buses standing in the water on the far side of the river, covered in netting.

'Yum!' Ditzy swam round in a little excited circle. 'Yum, yum, YUM!'

Lulu was sniffing the air. 'What is that marvellous smell?'

'It's a fish farm!' Ditzy bobbed about in the water and turned a sealy somersault. 'You see? Succulent salmon. Thousands of them! Salmon as far as the eye can see and the nose can smell.

Here you'll find salmon that are kept behind nets so they can't get out. All we have to do is get through the nets, swim in after them, and help ourselves. Chomp, chomp, CHOMPITY-CHOMP!'

'What?' Mr Dog's shaggy eyebrows shot upwards. 'No wonder the humans are upset,' he said. 'It's one thing to take fish that are swimming free in the river, but these fish belong to the farmers.'

'Do they?' Ditzy looked puzzled. 'Still, they won't mind me taking a few, surely?' Ditzy turned to Lulu. 'It's wonderful, Lu – you just push your snout in through the net and nibble!'

'As easy as that?' Lulu marvelled. 'No wonder you've stayed here so long.'

Ditzy nodded. 'The nets they use aren't all that strong, but they do have more than one layer. I've had to tear quite a few nets away to get to the fish inside.' She swam to some nearby reeds where some netting had snagged. 'This is the stuff they use. See, that's what got caught on the lid of the crate – it must have been washed away from here downriver . . .'

Mr Dog stared at the distinctive red mesh. 'Lulu, do you recognise that netting?'

Lulu quivered. 'I do – and I still have the

injuries to prove it. Oh, Ditzy – it was *your* fault I got stuck.'

Ditzy looked shaken. 'Mine?'

'Another one of these nets was washed downriver and I got tangled in it,' Lulu went on. 'I might've died if Mr Dog hadn't helped me.'

'Really? I'm so sorry. SO sorry.' Ditzy looked crestfallen, then brightened. 'Hey, let me get you some salmon to cheer you up!'

'Oh, Ditzy.' Mr Dog sighed. 'You've got so greedy for fish that you haven't stopped to think of the effect you're having on others.'

'It was only a few nets I tore free,' Ditzy argued. 'Humans cause most of the pollution here.'

'But we all have to live together as best we can,' said Mr Dog firmly. 'You've been too clever at stealing fish. It costs the farm owners money. They've tried to keep you out, but it hasn't worked so now they want to put a stop to the stealing for good – by putting a stop to you!'

'The hunters,' Lulu breathed. 'So *that's* why they're after us seals.'

She looked at Ditzy. Ditzy looked back at Lulu. Both seals lowered their heads.

'I'm sorry, Lu,' said Ditzy at last. 'I thought it was seal paradise here. I didn't mean to cause so many problems – or to hurt you.'

'I know you didn't,' Lulu said fondly. 'You're a friend. A mate. I've missed you.'

'I've missed you too,' said Ditzy.

'But the hunters won't miss *either* of you!' Mr Dog woofed, and his fur stood on end as a man with a rifle emerged from the bushes on the far side of the bank near the farming nets.

The man froze as he saw them. 'Two of you!' he declared. Then, carefully, he got into a nearby rowing boat.

'Hurry, we must get out of here,' Mr Dog hissed. But, as he turned to race back the way he'd come, he saw Alana the angler and another man heading towards them. The man was carrying a gun too.

'Oh no!' Lulu squealed. 'We're trapped!'

Chapter Eight

A DANGEROUS JOURNEY

As the people came closer, Mr Dog's mind was racing. 'Get up on the bank, you two,' he told the seals. 'Keep your heads down and follow me over the ground as fast as you can.'

Ditzy and Lulu hauled themselves out of the water and went galumphing after him at top speed. They would have looked comical, bouncing along like giant sausages, had the situation not been so dangerous.

'Where are we going?' Lulu panted.

'Look – all that rain has made a big pond on the far side of the railway tracks,' Mr Dog explained. 'You two can hide in there while I try to lead the hunters away.'

'It's us they want,' said Ditzy. 'They won't shoot a dog. You could get away.'

'Nonsense,' Mr Dog told her. 'I will do all I can to help you.'

'Why?' Ditzy asked.

'Because there's no "DON'T" in "DOG" –

only "DO". Mr Dog gave a doggy grin. 'And I DO
believe there's a way out of this – if we keep our
heads about us.'

The man in the boat had rowed to their side
of the river. A gunshot cracked out.

'Eeek!' Lulu tried to hurry, her poorly flipper
dragging behind her. 'I'd definitely like to keep
my head if at all possible!'

Mr Dog crossed over the railway tracks. He
squelched through the waterlogged grass to the
new pond, and the seals
did the same.

'In you go,' he urged.

Ditzy slithered in, but Lulu was exhausted. She had stopped for breath. Mr Dog barked furiously as Alana's friend and the man from the boat came striding towards the tracks, raising their guns . . .

Then, with a piercing whistle and a pounding of steel wheels, another goods train came thundering along – creating a heavy metal barrier between the hunters and the animals.

Mr Dog got behind Lulu and pushed her with both paws. She slid down over the wet grass and hit the water with a splash.

'Quickly!' said Ditzy, flippers flapping excitedly as the train rumbled along. 'I've explored. It's just a short hop from this pond into a ditch that leads back into the river.'

'That means we can double back behind the hunters,' Mr Dog realised. 'Good work, Ditzy. Come on!'

Mr Dog jumped into the water and did his best doggy-paddle alongside Lulu, keeping an eye on the tired seal as Ditzy led the way.

Ditzy rippled her body, sprang out of the pond

and into the

wet grassy ditch. 'Wheeeeee!'

She slid on her belly, back into the river like a

tubby torpedo.

Mr Dog let Lulu go first. Keeping low, he doggy-

paddled after the seals into the reeds and rushes

that fringed the river.

Together, the three animals swam downstream

as quickly as they could; Ditzy kept swimming

round behind Lulu and Mr Dog to chivvy them

along.

It was hard work swimming so fast, especially for

Mr Dog. 'I'm sorry,' he puffed. 'I need to rest.' He

climbed up on to the riverbank and shook himself.

The sun was out, and he was grateful for its warmth

as he lay on his side.

'That was close,' said Ditzy. 'Back in the harbour, people only took shots with their cameras!' She sighed. 'I've been a bad seal, haven't I?'

'You were only following your instincts,' said Mr Dog kindly. 'Seals will always want to eat fish. The farmers could make their nets stronger or their noisy machines better . . . but I'm afraid it's cheaper to deal with the seals.'

Lulu looked at Ditzy. 'I think it's time we returned to the sea.'

'I agree,' said Ditzy with feeling. 'But what if there are more hunters coming?'

Mr Dog nodded. 'Alana and her hunter friends

will catch us up for sure if we don't press on.'

'This is scary.' Lulu's eyes grew wider.
'Frightening. Petrifying!'

'I suggest we move on in stages.' Mr Dog got up and stretched. 'I'll go as far as the next bend by myself, check the way is clear – if it is, then I'll howl for you to join me.'

'We'll listen out,' said Lulu.

Ditzy bobbed and nodded in the water.
'Thank you, Mr Dog.' Then, with Lulu, she ducked out of sight.

Mr Dog ached from so much running and swimming, but, true to his woof, he scouted ahead at a fast trot, then howled to let the seals know it was safe to swim on. It was a long, exhausting afternoon. When another train went hurrying by, Mr Dog wished that he and the seals could jump on board for a free ride!

Evening was just beginning to steal the glow from the sky when Mr Dog met Ditzy and Lulu in the clearing where the train had gone off the rails. Mr Dog could see the net from the fish farm still trailing in the water, marking the spot where the crate lay submerged. If only he could do something about it!

'Please, Mr Dog, won't you rest?' said Lulu.

'I'm all right.' Mr Dog flopped down and yawned. 'I'm very fond of exercise.'

'I caught you a fish,' said Ditzy. 'I really wanted to eat it myself, but . . .'

'But it's good to think of others,' said Lulu with a nudge. 'Right, Ditzy?'

'Er, yes.' With a flick of her head, she tossed bits of fish up on to the bank. 'So I'd like you to have it.'

'That's kind, Ditzy. Thank you.' Though he was tired, Mr Dog gobbled down the fish with gusto. 'Now, I'd best check the way ahead again. You two stay here . . .' He walked on for thirty minutes or more, wishing his woofiest that there'd be no one in his way.

It was a wish that did not come true.

92

Round one corner, two people were crouched in the reeds beside the river. The evening sun glinted on the barrel of a rifle.

Mr Dog's blood ran cold. 'Hunters,' he growled. 'Hiding in the rushes . . . ready to set a trap!'

Chapter Nine

THE LAST HOPE

Keeping low on his belly, Mr Dog scuttled closer to the hunters, hoping to find out just what they were up to.

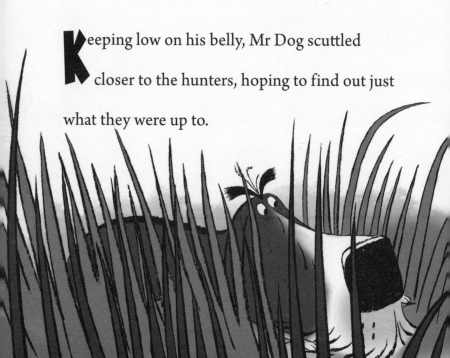

He heard one of the men speak: 'Poor little thing. Wonder how long it's been stuck in there.'

'Be careful not to hurt it,' said his friend. 'There's a split in the neck of the bottle. Try to open it up a bit . . .'

Mr Dog frowned. What on earth were these people up to? He crept closer and saw the men were gathered round a plastic juice bottle. A small animal – a vole or a mouse – had crawled inside and got stuck. There was no room for it to turn round. One of the men was carefully widening the split in the bottle, trying to let the animal out.

'There's so much pollution in this river.' The man with the rifle shook his head sadly. 'You know I'd rather be doing something about it than having to stop a hungry seal...'

It's not too late, old chap, thought Mr Dog as an idea struck him. *Perhaps – just perhaps – there's a way to make everyone happy!*

Carefully, he backed away through the long grass. The men would be busy for a little while – would he have long enough to carry out his plan? With alarm, he heard the *put-put-put* of an outboard engine and turned to find a small boat

96

in the distance, heading upriver towards the men in the reeds. There was a lantern on its prow. Was the boat carrying tourists on an evening jaunt, or were others coming to join the seal hunt . . .?

'There's not a moment to lose,' Mr Dog declared. Abandoning stealth, he darted off like a racehorse, scattering flies and dandelions as he covered the ground back to the clearing and the sunken crate.

'Ditzy! Lulu!' he woofed. 'Are you there?'

Lulu's head emerged from the water like a periscope. 'Is it safe?' she asked as Ditzy came up beside her.

'It won't be safe for long,' Mr Dog admitted.

'There are more hunters and a motorboat coming this way.'

Lulu gasped. 'And Alana and her two friends must still be after us from the other direction.'

'There's no way out,' said Ditzy sadly.

'There might be – if we can provide the right sort of distraction,' said Mr Dog. 'The hunters ahead of us were helping a vole trapped in a plastic bottle. I heard them say they want to do something about pollution in the river.'

'Don't we all,' said Lulu.

'So let's give them the chance.' Mr Dog ran down the bank to the water. 'That crate full of plastic packaging – what if we could show them it's here, and that it's leaking?'

Understanding dawned in Ditzy's dark eyes. 'You think the people would stop hunting us while they cleared up the mess?'

'Exactly,' Mr Dog declared. 'They care about this river and the fish in it, and the other animals affected. I think that they'll get to work at once.

And, while they're busy cleaning up the river, you seals can escape in the confusion.' He panted happily. 'It's a win-win situation!'

'But it'll be a *bang-bang* situation if we can't move that crate out of the water,' said Lulu. 'You know it's quite big and rather heavy . . .'

'So am I!' Ditzy boomed. 'Come on, Lu, let's try to push it.'

The two seals plopped into the river and Mr Dog dived after them. He tried to stand beside the crate on the riverbed and push with his front paws, but it was tricky – the seals were built to stay underwater and he was not.

Spluttering and gasping, Mr Dog returned

to the surface. 'I'll just have to keep watch,' he decided.

Minutes passed and the seals pushed and pulled and shoved at the crate. Mr Dog could see their shadows shifting beneath the water. The crate rocked back and forth but couldn't be budged.

Further down the river, the motorboat chugged slowly into sight.

'Ditzy, Lulu!' Mr Dog barked wildly. 'We don't have much time!'

'It's no good!' Lulu burst from the water, whiskers quivering. 'We can't move it.'

'It's stuck in the mud,' Ditzy added.

Mr Dog growled to see distant torchlights bobbing along the riverbank to his left – the men must have rescued the vole and were now continuing the hunt for Ditzy and Lulu. Then he saw torchlight to his right as well!

'We've got nowhere to go!' Lulu groaned. 'Our fate is sealed!'

'We'll have to swim for it, Lu,' said Ditzy. 'If we dive down, perhaps we can give them the slip.'

'They'll keep on coming,' said Lulu. 'We've been lucky so far, but the net is closing round us . . .'

'The net!' Mr Dog almost howled. 'Of course – the netting that's snagged on the crate's lid. Is it caught there good and tight?'

'Yes,' said Lulu. 'But how does that help us?'

'We can't move the crate,' said Mr Dog, 'but maybe we can *lift its lid*.'

'I see what you mean,' said Ditzy slowly. 'If we swing the lid open, it will stick out from the water . . .'

'And the hunters will know the crate's there without us having to move it!' Lulu finished.

'Precisely!' Mr Dog's tail wagged as hard as it would go. 'Ditzy, Lulu, you must each take an end of the net and wrap it round the edge of the lid. Then we can all pull up on it as hard as we can to lift it open. Quickly – before it's too late!'

Chapter Ten

SEALING THE DEAL

Mr Dog watched as the seals dipped beneath the water. The boat was chugging towards them now, as if drawn by the movement. The hunters, too, were quickening their step.

Ditzy and Lulu reappeared with one end of the net in their powerful jaws and clambered up on to the bank. 'The net is in position,' Lulu reported.

'Excellent,' said Mr Dog, scrambling down to join them. 'With any luck by pulling on the net we'll pull up the lid too. We have to force it all the way open so it can be seen.' He grabbed some of the net in his own jaws. 'Mmmm, I do love a good tug toy!'

Lulu and Ditzy began to heave, and Mr Dog dug his front paws into the ground and pulled on the net with all his might. The lid began to creak. *Come on,* he thought as the seals strained even harder beside him, and the creaking grew deeper and louder. *Together we can do it ... We* have *to do it!*

Finally – *CRACK!* The damaged crate lid snapped open on its twisted hinges.

Mr Dog and the seals let go of the net and were sent tumbling backwards.

'Success!' squealed Lulu.

'Well done, you two,' Mr Dog panted, rolling on to one side. The white lid was now standing straight up from the water like toast from a toaster. 'All right now – dive! Stay out of sight.'

'We'll do our best,' Ditzy promised, before she and Lulu slid like jumbo sausages back into the river.

Both groups of hunters were converging on Mr Dog now, but he was too exhausted to move. He lay there panting as they closed in.

'It's that mutt again!' came a man's voice as

torch beams played over him.

'It's John Tregeen's dog, from down in the town.' Mr Dog recognised the voice of Alana the angler. 'It is, I'm sure of it.'

'You're right there, Alana,' came a deep, familiar voice from the motorboat as the engine died away. 'Hello, boy! Fancy seeing you here.'

Mr Dog jumped up. Could it be . . .?

YES! It was John Tregeen in the boat, with Sadiq from his fishing crew holding the lantern!

Mr Dog clambered into the boat and yapped happily around John's legs. 'It's good to see you,' he woofed.

John kneeled down and fussed Mr Dog.

'When Alana told me you'd been seen with seals and a hunting party was after them, I got worried and came looking.'

I've been quite worried myself, thought Mr Dog. But he couldn't make John understand that, so he settled for giving him a lick or two.

'I'm glad you've got your dog back, John,' said Alana. 'Now, please take him away, before he leads us another merry dance.'

'Thanks for tipping me off that he was here, Alana,' John said, then frowned as Sadiq shone his light on the upstanding lid of the crate. 'What *is* that?'

'A big box, by the look of it,' said Vole-Saving Man. 'What's inside?'

110

'Let's check it out,' said Alana. 'Is that plastic packaging?'

'It must have come off that train that derailed here a few weeks back,' said John. 'If this gets washed out, there'll be enough to keep the beach clean-up team busy for weeks!'

'What about the seals?' said one of the other men impatiently. 'They're what we came out to deal with.'

'Forget them for now,' said Vole-Saving Man. 'If they're gone, they're gone. We need to get this thing out of the water and dispose of it properly.'

'I'll give you a hand,' said John, jumping from the boat to the riverbank.

All attention was now fixed on the problematic

crate – except, of course, for Mr Dog's. He was

busy watching two dark, slippery shapes glide

away through the water, vanishing into the night.

Sadiq noticed too, smiled, and looked at Mr Dog

with a finger to his lips, as if to say, 'Keep quiet!'

I will, thought Mr Dog. *Nothing good can come out of that crate, but great things will come from this evening's work – that's for sure!*

*

Mr Dog was so tired out that he fell asleep in John's boat. When his eyes flickered open again, the boat was being steered back down the river by John and Sadiq, the outboard motor grumbling away.

John smiled. 'You look worn out, boy. I am too, after helping to shift that wretched crate out of the water. Still, at least it can't harm the environment any more. It'll be recycled and disposed of properly.'

Thank goodness for that, thought Mr Dog. He looked out into the black night. *I wonder where Ditzy and Lulu are now . . . Did they make it back home to the sea?*

The hours passed and the boat finally reached the estuary where the river met the sea. The harbour was still dark, but the jetty was lit by strings of white fairy lights, waving in a breeze

blowing in from the sea. In the glow that they

spilled, Mr Dog saw two grey weighty sausage

shapes bobbing about. Could it be . . .?

'Lulu! Ditzy!' Mr Dog put his paws up on the

side of the boat and barked at them. 'You made

it! You're all right!'

'We are now, Mr Dog!' Lulu called back. 'Free.

Safe. Together.'

'I'm going to teach Lulu how to put on a show here in the harbour,' said Ditzy. 'She does an excellent impression of a log, you know.'

'I've seen it,' woofed Mr Dog.

'I reckon we'll get all sorts of extra snacks as a double act,' Lulu said. 'And I'm sure Ditzy will even share some with the shyer seals . . .'

'I suppose,' Ditzy grumbled.

'You two are good for each other.' Mr Dog gave his widest doggy grin. 'Good luck!'

John looked over and laughed. 'I'm glad to see Ditzy back,' he told Sadiq. 'The locals love her, and the tourists will come looking for her when they hear. We ought to sell more fish than ever.' He grinned. 'Wasn't it funny the way the dog barked at the seals and they grunted back? You could almost believe they were talking to each other . . .'

The men laughed, but Mr Dog just smiled to himself. He knew that his work here was done.

John crouched beside his canine companion. 'You know, boy, I have a feeling your real home is out there on the open road. You're all about finding new friends and fresh adventures . . . Am I right?' He smiled and stroked Mr Dog's neck. 'Still, before you head off again, how about you rest at my place for a couple of days and let me feed you up a bit, eh?' He held out his hand. 'Do we have a deal?'

I believe we do, kind sir! thought Mr Dog.

He solemnly held out his paw, which John

took and shook, and somewhere in the harbour,

Lulu and Ditzy barked their approval.

There, thought Mr Dog, *the deal is SEALED. A*

little rest, a lot of food – and then off I go again!

Notes from the Author

I have always loved seals. The first time I met one in the wild, I was on a rough boat trip to the remote Scottish island of Eigg in the Inner Hebrides. It was Easter and the seas were mountainous. I was only ten and it all seemed a little scary . . . until I noticed some little black heads with their beady eyes staring up from the rough waters. As my eyes adjusted, I noticed dozens of them. My enduring love for seals was sealed.

When on Taransay island for a year, my Labrador, Inca, used to leap into the freezing Hebridean water and play hide-and-seek. Have you ever noticed how much seals resemble Labradors? Sometimes I couldn't tell mammal and dog apart. My most enduring memory, however, is of Nelson, the famous one-eyed seal of Looe in Devon, which inspired me to put the statue in chapter one. Nelson was the most famous resident of Looe for more than twenty-five years and I often saw him in the harbour. The fishermen would throw him fish and people travelled from far and wide to watch. When he died, there was such mourning that a bronze statue was erected in his memory. Seals have a way of looking into your soul with those big doleful eyes, just like Lulu does in the story. I'll always love seals. Reassuringly, they remind me of my childhood.

How to help with plastic

Plastic rubbish is littering our oceans and threatening the lives of millions of marine animals around the world. Seals are curious creatures and can get caught in fishing nets, plastic waste and discarded rubbish. We all have to do our bit to help protect these animals and keep our oceans healthy.

When you can, try to say no to single-use plastics. Don't use plastic straws, and ask your parents to bring their own bags when they go shopping. If you do have to use plastic, make sure you clean up after yourself. If you go to the beach or to the park, don't drop your rubbish on the sand or on the grass! Look for a recycling bin or, if there isn't one around, take it home and recycle it there. We can make clothes, shoes and all sorts of other things out of recycled plastic, which is so much better than it ending up in the ocean.

Read on for a sneak peek of
Mr Dog's next adventure,

Chapter One

CRATES AND CASES

It was a bright but chilly April afternoon. A hard sea wind huffed at the ferryboat as it braved the waves off the craggy coast of Scotland.

The people on the ferryboat had no idea that a stowaway had crept on board: a furry, four-legged, rather scruffy stowaway, who was now hiding below deck in the cargo hold! Aside from his white beard, his fur was dark and shaggy. A ragged red-and-white hanky was tied about his neck. His ears were floppy, his nose was large and his brown eyes sparkled even in the gloom.

He wasn't just a dog. He was *Mr Dog*.

Mr Dog was a big fan of adventures so he'd been roaming all over, from the south of England way up to the highlands of Scotland. It was there that he'd spied a group of people in a pretty little town catching the ferryboat to some islands off the coast, so he had crept into the cargo hold to go with them, and now here he was!

To his surprise, he had found the hold mostly full of animal crates and carriers – at least forty of them. From the smell, he could tell that they had been used very recently. Some of them still had a few crushed dog biscuits inside (although with a hungry Mr Dog around, not for long). The funny thing, though, was that the crates didn't smell of dogs or cats or even of rabbits or rats, but of another animal – one that Mr Dog couldn't quite recognise. Someone had left a little fresh water in some of the bowls, so Mr Dog was glad for that.

Finally, the ferryboat slowed as it neared its destination, and Mr Dog felt the usual thrill of excitement of being about to explore somewhere new. 'Now, how to get off without being seen?' he mused.

Just then, the door to the hold was thrown open. Mr Dog ducked inside a pet carrier with solid plastic sides as a lady in a bright-red coat with frizzy blonde hair bustled inside. 'I can see Jed's pick-up truck waiting,' the lady called to one of the crew. 'He'll help me unload the empty crates.'

'Right you are, Lizzie,' a woman called back.

How kind of this Jed to help Lizzie – and to help

me too! thought Mr Dog. *I may as well stay in here*

and be carried off in style . . .

Sure enough, once the boat had moored up,

Jed came aboard and helped frizzy-haired Lizzie

shift the crates and cages off the boat. It took

several trips. Mr Dog held his breath as his own

carrier was lifted up.

'This one weighs a ton!' Jed declared.

How dare you! thought Mr Dog with a secret

chuckle.

As soon as the crate was put down, Mr Dog cautiously nosed open the door of his carrier and peered out. He was in the back of Jed's pick-up truck, which was as red as Lizzie's coat, and parked on a pier beside a small rocky harbour. Suddenly, he heard angry voices from beside a dark-green van parked close by. Lizzie was arguing with another woman whose sharp features reminded Mr Dog of a hunting bird, and he raised his ears to listen in.

'If I'd known you were only going over to the mainland to bring back more spotlights, Mrs

Maitland, I'd have thrown them overboard!' said Lizzie hotly. 'What you've been doing to those hedgies is plain cruel!'

Mr Dog was puzzled. 'Cruelty to hedgies?' he murmured. 'Whatever does she mean?'

Mrs Maitland remained calm and haughty. 'They don't belong on the Isle of Evan, Lizzie. We'll get rid of them a lot faster by hunting them down than by taking them over to the mainland in crates . . .'

'Rubbish!' Lizzie insisted. 'Your hunts are dangerous and unnecessary and they're going to stop, mark my words.'

'Are they indeed!' Mrs Maitland sneered.

'Is a hedgie like a hedge?' Mr Dog wondered

aloud. (Although to humans, of course, it came

out as Grrr, wuff-wuff RUFF!) He jumped down

from Jed's pick-up truck and trotted past the

other side of Mrs Maitland's green van, shaking

his head. 'I should think it is unnecessary to hunt

down a hedge – it just stands there and lets you

find it!'

'They're not talking about hedges.' A large,

sturdy tan basset hound in a thick leather collar

leaned through the van window. 'They're talking

about hedgehogs.'

'Hedgehogs!' Mr Dog grinned. 'Of course,

that was the smell in those cages. Wait a

moment. Why are hedgehogs being taken to the

mainland? Why don't they belong on this island?'

'Who cares?' said the basset hound. 'If Mrs

Maitland says they don't, then they don't. She's

my mistress, after all.'

'So Mrs Maitland is hunting these hedgies?'

'No, dogs like me are hunting them.' The

basset hound looked confused. 'Aren't you

hunting them too?'

'Goodness, no! The only things I'm hunting are happy memories.' He raised a paw. 'I'm Mr Dog, by the way.'

'My name's Dandy.' The basset hound looked suspiciously at Mr Dog. 'I've never seen you before on the island. Did you come over from the mainland with Lizzie? Or "Lizzie Toddy, Busybody" as my mistress calls her.'

Mr Dog was not impressed by name-calling. 'I did come over from the mainland,' he said. 'But not with Lizzie. I just cadged a lift in the boat.'

'Well, perhaps you'd like to join us on the hunt tonight?' said Dandy. 'It's a good chase with all the other sniffer dogs, plus it's even more fun in the dark.'

'So that's why you need the spotlights! Hedgehogs only come out at night.' Mr Dog sighed. He always felt sorry for an underdog – or an under*hog* in this case. 'Well, thanks for the invite to the hunt, but no thanks. I hope it all goes wonderfully well . . .' As he turned, he added quietly: 'for the hedgehogs!'

'I heard that!' Dandy's hackles rose. 'Well, just

make sure you stay out of the way of my hunting pals and me . . . and don't make friends with any hedgies if you know what's good for you.'

'Perhaps I should change my name to Mr *Doog*?' Mr Dog grinned. 'Then I'd know what's good for me backwards!'

By now, Mrs Maitland had loaded her spotlights into her van and was clambering into the driver's seat beside Dandy. 'Stop grumbling, boy!' She snapped at his low growls. 'I'm the one who should grumble, having to deal with Lizzie Toddy, busybody . . .'

Dandy barked an 'I told you so' at Mr Dog. Then the van's engine started and Mr Dog scampered away. Mrs Maitland and Dandy drove off, then Lizzie and Jed drove away in the opposite direction.

Mr Dog trotted up the nearest grassy hillside to take a good look around at his surroundings and plan his next steps. But, really, he already knew what he was going to do.

'It sounds like the Isle of Evan's hedgies could use a good friend,' he declared. 'Luckily, good friends don't come any shaggier or waggier than Mr Dog!'